ENEMIES

By the same author

Games
Hating Alison Ashley
People Might Hear You
Penny Pollard's Letters
Penny Pollard's Diary

ENEMIES
ROBIN KLEIN

illustrated by

NOELA YOUNG

Cover illustration by Donna Roff

A
LITTLE APPLE
PAPERBACK

SCHOLASTIC INC.

New York   Toronto   London   Auckland   Sydney

ISBN 0-590-43689-9

Text copyright © 1985 by Haytul Pty Ltd.
Illustrations copyright © 1985 by Angus & Robertson Publishers.
All rights reserved. Published by Scholastic Inc., 730 Broadway,
New York, NY 10003 by arrangement with E. P. Dutton, a division of
Penguin Books USA Inc.
APPLE PAPERBACKS is a registered trademark of Scholastic Inc.

12 11 10 9 8 7 6 5 4 3   1 2 3 4 5/9

Printed in the U.S.A.

First Scholastic printing, November 1990

Contents

1 The Enemies

Mary-Anna Clutterworth's mother and Sandra Sutton's mother were very good friends. They went to yoga class together on Wednesday mornings, and they both worked part-time as nurses at the same hospital. They had morning coffee at each other's houses and borrowed extra glasses, recipes, and earrings when they had parties. And not once in the ten years they had been living two streets apart had they had the slightest argument.

But Mary-Anna Clutterworth and Sandra Sutton absolutely hated each other. They were in the same class at school, and every few weeks their teacher made everyone move to different desks and sit next to different people. That's how Mary-Anna and Sandra came to be sitting next to each other, because they certainly wouldn't have chosen to do so otherwise.

They both put on sulky faces and muttered while they were moving their things into the same desk one rainy lunchtime. Sandra wasn't very neat. She had scribbly drawings on computer paper, nibbled rulers, old potato-chip bags, a dried starfish, parts from a handmade mobile that had crash-landed, fifty-seven trading cards, and dozens of felt pens that had all died.

Mary-Anna frowned when she saw all of Sandra's junk spilling like the contents of a dump truck into the desk. "Keep that junk on your side," she said, outraged. "This desk isn't a garbage can or the town dump."

Sandra shoved in some jar lids filled with smelly cotton wool and bean sprouts, two compasses that didn't work anymore, and a pair of damp socks. She banged her lunch box down on the desk, opened it, and looked around, ignoring Mary-Anna completely.

Two could play at that game, thought Mary-Anna. She took out the wonderful new pencil sharpener her Uncle Jason had brought back from Canada. It was made like a little miniature sawmill, only instead of cutting logs, it shaved pencils to a nice sharp point. She was the only kid in Glendale Primary who had such a neat pencil sharpener. Now she sharpened all her pencils at both ends. The shavings rained like a multicolored cloudburst over Sandra's open lunch box. Sandra was having an egg-and-lettuce salad that day. She certainly wasn't very pleased about having a garnish of pencil shavings.

"All right, Mary-Anna Clutterworth!" she hissed. "I'm going to get you after school for doing that!"

But after school, Mary-Anna went and climbed right up to the top of the jungle gym. She knew that she was safe there, because Sandra didn't like climbing high things and wouldn't dare come after her. Sandra stood at the foot of the jungle gym and shook the steel bars fiercely, as though Mary-Anna were a plum in a tree.

"Why don't you climb up here and get me?" Mary-Anna teased. "You're too scared, that's why."

"You're too scared to climb down here, you mean," said Sandra.

"I don't have to if I don't want to. I like it up here," Mary-Anna said, and did two expert back flips. Sandra shook the bars some more, but she couldn't hang around being a bully because she had to go to an exercise class instead. Mary-Anna's book bag and raincoat and pom-pom hat were lying on the ground, and Sandra was so angry that she snatched up the hat and ran off with it.

Mary-Anna's mother was very annoyed with her for not having the hat when she got home.

"I didn't lose it," Mary-Anna said. "That

horrible Sandra Sutton took it. She belongs in a reform school."

"What nonsense," said her mother. "Sandra wouldn't steal anything. She's a darling little girl. You just hunt through the lost-and-found box tomorrow at school, miss, and don't come home without that hat."

Mary-Anna waited until her mother had left for the night shift at the hospital, then she called Sandra. "You might think you're smart, Sandra," she said threateningly, "but oh, boy, are you going to get into trouble!"

"I don't know what you mean," Sandra said airily.

"Oh yes you do!"

"Oh no I don't."

"You certainly do! You'd just better have my new pom-pom hat with you at school tomorrow, that's all! That pom-pom hat cost three dollars and fifty cents at Tinker's."

"Only little kids in first grade wear hats from Tinker's," said Sandra. "I certainly wouldn't be seen wearing a little kid's hat from Tinker's. I don't know anyone else who would, either. My goodness, do you really buy your hats from the little kids' department at Tinker's? Everyone else in the class is going to be very interested to hear about that when I tell them."

"I'll get my mom to call your mom," Mary-Anna said, but Sandra only laughed rudely and hung up. She knew that their mothers never took any notice of her and Mary-Anna fighting. "And if you don't bring it back, I'm going to get you tomorrow, Sandra Sutton!" Mary-Anna said into the empty phone. She didn't exactly know how, because although Sandra was scared of heights, she was a very good fighter.

In the morning, Mary-Anna checked the hooks outside the classroom, but Sandra hadn't put back the pom-pom hat. Mary-Anna went hunting for her like a warrior looking for revenge and found Sandra helping the librarian unpack books. Mary-Anna stood in the doorway and glared horribly at

Sandra and said, *"Where is my hat?"* without making a sound. The librarian turned around and glanced in surprise at her twisting mouth, and Mary-Anna felt terribly embarrassed and let it go flat and normal again.

Sandra carried a stack of books to the desk near the door and said loudly, "You'll have to get out of the way, Mary-Anna. People aren't allowed to clutterworth up the doorway." She picked up a rubber stamp and began to stamp the books importantly, and she smiled at Mary-Anna with a smile that wasn't one really; it was more of a deadly insult without words. "I found a funny little pom-pom hat near the jungle gym yesterday," she said. "I thought some teeny-weeny kid in kindergarten must own it, so I put it on their hooks. It's exactly the same pattern as those teeeeeny-weeeeeny little kids wear."

"All right, then," said Mary-Anna. "Just for that, I want that camel necklace back I gave you for your birthday. I only gave it to

you because my mom said I had to give you a present. I certainly wouldn't have given you anything on my own. Or if I did, it would have been a run-over frog or a jigsaw puzzle with a whole lot of pieces missing. You just bring that camel necklace back tomorrow, or else!"

"I don't want that old necklace, anyhow," said Sandra. "I never wear it. I never liked it in the first place. I'll have a hard job finding it, because I just threw it into the bottom of the sewing basket at home so I wouldn't even have to look at it."

It was an unusual necklace made of wooden camels threaded together, and Sandra really did like it. She wore it to places where she was sure that Mary-Anna wouldn't see her. Next day in the corridor she pulled it out of her bag and said, "Here's your stupid-looking old camel necklace, and good riddance!" She had to turn her head away while she gave it back, because parting with it hurt very much. It was made of sandalwood and had an interesting, sweaty smell, and all the camels had different expressions. She had given them names such as Abdul, Ali, and Mohammed.

Mary-Anna didn't feel as triumphant as she thought she would at getting the necklace back. A girl called Julie O'Hara came up and admired it. "You can have it to keep, if you like," Mary-Anna said, and Julie fastened it around her neck and ran around showing everyone in the room. Mary-Anna glanced secretly at Sandra to see if she minded, but Sandra was busily drawing horses on her folder cover and coloring them in, and she didn't even look up.

"That necklace looks fantastic on you, Julie," Mary-Anna said in a very loud voice. "And it comes from overseas, too. My Uncle Jason bought it on a business trip to Cairo." Sandra just went on filling in an orange-outlined horse purple, but some of the pur-

ple went over the orange lines, and although she was humming to herself, the humming sounded bothered and wobbly.

At lunchtime they had to eat inside because it was raining again. Sandra had a hot lunch from the cafeteria, and Mary-Anna looked at her own peanut-butter-and-celery sandwiches and thought they were very boring. Sandra had a meat pie and a glazed doughnut and a delicious frozen strawberry ice pop. Mary-Anna looked sideways at the pie and the doughnut and the ice pop laid out on the desk, and bit unenthusiastically into her peanut-butter-and-celery sandwich. Sometimes people who had hot lunches generously let their best friends have a bite, but Sandra was her enemy.

"Do you want some of my pie, Julie?" Sandra asked, and Julie looked delighted. "You can have half my doughnut, too, and first bite of the strawberry ice pop," said Sandra. She kept passing those wonderful things back and forth, right under Mary-Anna's nose, and each time Mary-Anna nearly choked on her healthy peanut-butter-and-celery sandwich on whole wheat. But she didn't let Sandra see that she cared one bit.

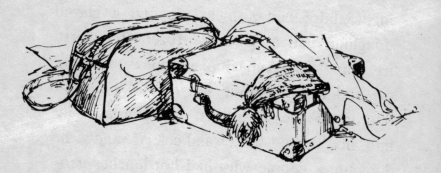

2 "That Horse Is Crazy"

When it stopped raining, they all went outside to play. Mary-Anna went right to the bars, where she could do complicated tricks. Usually she had a crowd of girls all wanting her to show them how to do those tricks, too. Sandra never played on the bars because she was clumsy and scared of heights. She played sevens against the wall of the equipment shed instead. She had to play it all by herself, because everyone liked the bars best.

Mary-Anna glanced down and thought Sandra looked lonely all by herself. "Hey," she called, because she felt ashamed and guilty that she had asked for a birthday present back. "Sandra, if you come up here, I'll show you how to hang by your legs." She didn't make her voice sound either friendly or unfriendly, but Sandra looked up suspiciously, thinking she was just showing off.

"You couldn't teach anyone anything except how to suck their thumb. You're the world's expert at that, Mary-Anna Clutterworth," she said coldly.

Mary-Anna blushed, because she still did suck her thumb when she was tired or watching something interesting on TV. She knew she was too old to suck her thumb, and she hated to be reminded of it. She was so annoyed that she made a lot of insulting remarks about how stupid Sandra was on the jungle gym, and how she couldn't even do the simplest trick. And how she had once got stuck halfway, and Mr. Morley, their teacher, had had to come out of the teachers' room and coax her down. It had taken a very long time. Some of the other girls joined in the teasing and pretended to be Sandra, stuck, bawling, halfway up the bars, and the others pretended to be Mr. Morley on the ground, patiently trying to get her to stop howling and unclamp her fingers and climb down. Sandra scowled, stopped bouncing the ball against the equipment shed, and went away. But first she yelled, "I'll get you for that, Mary-Anna Clutterworth! This afternoon!"

In the afternoon, Mary-Anna was called up to the front of the class to read aloud. Mr. Morley was standing at the back of the room, and Sandra kept making terrible faces at Mary-Anna whenever she looked up from the book. But Mary-Anna couldn't make one back. Then Sandra leaned forward and whispered something to Mark Hunter. Mark Hunter grinned and whispered something to Philip Spence, who sat next to him, and the whisper trickled right around the room, from desk to desk.

Mary-Anna read to the bottom of the page and looked up. Everyone in the room, except Mr. Morley, had their thumbs in their mouths. They were sitting up nicely and listening to the reading, but they were all sucking their thumbs and staring at her, smirking around the edges of their wet thumbs.

Mr. Morley said, "Go on reading, Mary-Anna. Why have you stopped?"

Mary-Anna turned red and stumbled over a lot of words she knew perfectly well. Each time she looked up, everyone stared at her with dancing eyes, with their thumbs tucked into their mouths, and dimples popping in and out of their cheeks, if they had dimples. When she finished reading, Sandra shot her a gloating look and took her thumb out and wiped it dry on a tissue.

"Just you wait, Sandra Sutton!" Mary-Anna hissed when she sat down. "I'm going to pay you back for that!"

Mr. Morley always took them for a nature-study walk once a week. All the girls fought to be the ones to walk on either side of him,

but Sandra never did if Mary-Anna was already on one side, and Mary-Anna never did if Sandra was.

When they walked past Mary-Anna's house, Sandra said loudly, "That's where that stupid Mary-Anna Clutterworth lives. Just look at her bedroom curtains! They're pink, and they've got little rabbits and ducks all over them. What a baby!"

So when they passed by Sandra's house, Mary-Anna said, to get her back, "That's Sandra's room there at the front, and just look at that row of dolls on the window ledge! She takes them to bed with her every night and sings them to sleep!"

Sandra didn't, because they were a collection of ornamental dolls in national dress, so she hit Mary-Anna, and Mary-Anna hit her back. Mr. Morley made them separate and walk one at the front of the line and one at the end. He took the class down to the highway excavations and let them watch the earth-moving equipment, which wasn't really nature study, but everyone liked it, and so did Mr. Morley.

When it was time to go back to school, they took a shortcut across a paddock. There was a very quiet, old brown horse grazing in the paddock. It stared at them all when they walked through, and tossed its head and whinnied and ran nervously back and forth.

"Just keep walking," Mr. Morley said. "Don't frighten the poor old thing."

Mary-Anna wasn't worried about frightening the horse, because horses always scared *her* into a tremble. She squealed loudly when it trotted toward them, and Mr. Morley told her not to be silly. Sandra wasn't a bit scared. She tugged out a tuft of grass and tried to coax the horse to come and take it from her hand. She moved close to Mary-Anna so Mr. Morley couldn't hear what she was saying.

"Hey, Mary-Anna," she whispered. "That

horse is crazy. I heard it went for a kid and stepped on her foot and wouldn't get off. Yes, that horse certainly has got crazy, dangerous eyes. He seems to be heading over here, too. Maybe he's interested in *you*! They had to get a bulldozer to make the horse get off that other kid's foot. She was trapped for four days."

Mary-Anna yelped and rushed over to Mr. Morley and grabbed his sleeve. He was holding a strand of barbed wire up so the children could get through the fence, but Mary-Anna didn't notice that. She had shut her eyes so she wouldn't see the horse's crazy ones. She just grabbed in a panic at Mr. Morley, and his sleeve got tangled up in the barbed wire. She thought she heard him say a word they always got into trouble for saying in the playground, and she opened her eyes and stared at him in surprise.

Mr. Morley was wearing a marvelous hand-knit sweater, which had cost over

ninety dollars, and he wasn't very pleased that now the sleeve of it was snarled and tangled up in the barbed-wire fence.

"You can't come on any more of our nature-study walks, Mary-Anna, if you're going to be so hysterical," he said indignantly. "We can all see that horse is harmless. Look, Sandra's just standing there petting him."

Sandra was feeding the horse the tuft of grass and leaning against him cozily as

though he were a telephone booth. Mary-Anna slunk through the fence and got into line with everyone, and they all looked at her as though she belonged in a baby carriage. They had to wait a long time while Mr. Morley unraveled a lot of his sweater from the barbed wire and wound the expensive hand-spun wool into a ball. Mary-Anna thought that every dropped stitch was her fault.

She was too upset to tell Sandra that she would get her on the way home from school. "I just won't have anything more to do with Sandra Sutton ever again!" she decided furiously.

But when she got home, her mother was packing things into a suitcase. "Dad and I have to fly to Sydney for the weekend," she said. "Uncle Jason is getting married tomorrow instead of next month, because he has to go overseas again unexpectedly. Sandra's mother said you can stay with them till we get back."

"Why can't I come to Sydney and stay with Grandma?" Mary-Anna cried.

"You can't, darling. I'm sorry. Grandma's got a big crowd of relatives she has to put up at short notice. There just won't be any room at all. Not even for an air mattress on the living-room floor."

"But I don't want to stay at Sandra's!" Mary-Anna wailed. "I hate her. I'd rather stay here by myself. I could do that, couldn't I, Mom? I promise I won't watch anything bloodthirsty on television, and I won't open the door to strangers, and I won't eat messy things like spaghetti and meatballs in bed."

"Of course you couldn't stay here alone. Don't be silly, Mary-Anna, and don't nag and pester, either. I'm in a terrible rush, and trying to do hundreds of things at once. A button's come off Dad's good suit, and I can't find one to match. And you'll have to do a bit of rushing yourself. Get a nightie and all the things you'll need for Sandra's,

and put them in your bag. We'll drop you off there when we leave for the airport."

Mary-Anna sulkily packed some games that only one person could play, because she didn't want or intend to have anything to do with Sandra over the weekend. She signed the card her mother had bought to go with the wedding gift and added *Best wishes for future happiness*, though she secretly blamed the bride and groom for spoiling her weekend. If it hadn't been nice Uncle Jason getting married, she could have almost wished that he and his bride would fight a lot, or get confetti in their eyes, or receive boring presents they didn't like or already had.

Her parents dropped her off at Sandra's, and Mrs. Sutton opened the door. Mary-Anna tried to wriggle the frown off her face and look happy because Mrs. Sutton was really nice. It wasn't her fault that she had Sandra for a child.

3 A Nice Game of Monopoly

"Put your things in Sandra's room," Mrs. Sutton said, smiling at Mary-Anna. "Won't it be great fun, sleeping here for the weekend? Sandra's looking forward to it." Which wasn't true at all, because Sandra had sulked and carried on in a very bad-tempered way when her mother had gotten the phone message. And then Sandra had rushed about hiding all her good things so Mary-Anna couldn't play with them. She had even eaten half a carton of chocolate ripple ice cream left over in the freezer, so there wouldn't be any to offer Mary-Anna. She was sitting on her bed, reading, and she didn't look up or say anything.

"Sandra," said her mother crossly, "it's very rude to ignore visitors. Say hello to Mary-Anna at once."

"I saw her all day at school, unfortunately," Sandra said. She glared over the top of her book, and Mary-Anna glared back.

"Well, then," Mrs. Sutton said rather helplessly. "I'll finish cooking dinner. You two try to play nicely together till it's ready, and don't fight. You could have a nice game of Monopoly."

Sandra waited until her mother was safely in the kitchen, then said fiercely, "Don't you lay a finger on anything of mine in this room. Especially not my Monopoly set."

"I wouldn't want to, even if I had plastic gloves on," said Mary-Anna. "I brought along my own things. And don't you dare touch them." She dug in her bag and pulled out a wonderful set of little playing cards in a leather box, which her Uncle Jason had sent her from Italy. She made a great show of shuffling them and spreading them out for a game of solitaire on the spare bed in Sandra's room. They didn't have just an ordinary scribbly pattern on their backs, like regular old playing cards. They had sweet little pictures of old-time people bringing in the harvest. Sandra, she was pleased to notice, was casting jealous looks at her playing cards.

Mary-Anna played one game of solitaire and put the cards back in their leather case. Then she felt in her case again and pulled out a magnificent wooden puzzle her Uncle Jason had sent her from Hong Kong. It was a flat box containing sliding, painted pieces of wood. Mary-Anna didn't really play with it very much, because she had never been able to work it out. But she pushed the wooden pieces into various positions, saying "*Hmmmm*" and "Let's see now," making it look as fascinating as possible so that Sandra would be jealous.

Sandra had put down her library book and was watching openly, looking as though she would soon ask if she could have a turn.

"No, you can't," said Mary-Anna when she did.

"It's rude not to share," Sandra said.

"What about you and your old Monopoly set, then?"

"I'll only let you play Monopoly if you let me work out that puzzle."

"No one can work out this puzzle. Especially not you. It's too hard."

"I bet you anything I can. I'm good at puzzles."

"Not this one. No one has ever worked it out, not in three hundred and eighty-five years. They've sent it to university teachers and computers all over the world, and nobody has worked it out yet."

"Phooey," said Sandra. "If I don't work it out, you can keep my Monopoly set, and if I do work it out, then I'm allowed to keep that old puzzle."

"All right, then, smarty," said Mary-Anna. She knew that Sandra had no chance. No kid she had shown it to had ever been able to work it out, not even Tracey Wang, and you'd think she'd be able to, seeing she was the smartest kid on their street.

Sandra came and sat next to Mary-Anna on the spare bed so she couldn't be accused of cheating. She slid the oblongs of wood sideways and up and down, and then she said triumphantly, "There! Just think, I'm the only person for three hundred and eighty-five years to work it out! You said so yourself. I *told* you I could work it out. So now it's mine."

Mary-Anna stared at the solved puzzle, with all the pieces where the instruction card said they should be. She swallowed hard as she watched Sandra put it away in a bedside thing she had that said RIBBONS, SOCKS, TREASURES on different pockets. Sandra removed everything else from the TREASURES section and put the puzzle in there by itself.

Then she hummed airily through a satisfied smirk.

"All right," Mary-Anna said angrily. "Let's play Monopoly. And if I win three games in a row, I can keep your Monopoly set."

"And if you lose, I'm allowed to keep those playing cards in the little leather box," said Sandra. "You might as well hand them over now and save time. I always beat everyone at Monopoly, including my dad, even though he's a real-estate salesman."

"We'll see about that," said Mary-Anna, and they sat on the floor and played Monopoly until Sandra's mother called them for dinner. Mary-Anna enjoyed the meal because she was already the owner of all four railroads and several properties with houses on them. Sandra had spent a lot of time being sent to jail, or landing on CHANCE, or paying rent.

"Do you girls want to watch TV?" Mrs. Sutton asked. "You can eat your apple pie in front of the set if you like. I'm sorry there's no ice cream to go with it. I could have sworn there was half a carton of chocolate ripple left in the freezer."

"We haven't got time for dessert," Sandra said grimly. "We're in the middle of a Monopoly game."

Mary-Anna won the first game easily. She tipped all her houses, hotels, and money back into the bank and smiled. "That was just like taking candy from a baby," she purred. "And now I'll win the second game."

The next game was interrupted when Mrs. Sutton told them they had to take showers and get ready for bed. But she said they could play for a little while after that.

"You'll have to come and sit in the bathroom while I take my shower, Mary-Anna," Sandra said. "I'm not going to leave you alone with the Monopoly set. I don't trust you. You'll steal a whole lot of five-hundred-dollar bills and say you had them all along."

"I certainly don't have to cheat to win," Mary-Anna said smugly. "Other people might have to, though."

They each took a rapid shower, and Mary-Anna noticed that Sandra had a bubble pipe and a plastic whale and a red ferryboat on the edge of the tub. "All these funny little bath toys are in the way," she said. "Have you had a little kid staying at your house? I wonder if he knows he left his toys behind?"

Sandra looked very annoyed, and Mary-Anna smirked to herself while she put on her new nightie. She was very proud because she had decorated it herself. One rainy Saturday she had cut out a green felt dragon and sewn it on the front. A red-and-orange-felt flame curved all the way down to the hem. The dragon's scales were green sequins, and its eyes were little round beads, which were a bit uncomfortable to lie on. Mary-Anna liked her nightie decorations very much and thought it might be nice to have someone other than a parent admire them. Sandra looked sideways at the nightie but didn't say anything.

When they finished the second game of Monopoly, which Mary-Anna won, she said, "I'm not so sorry now that I had to come and stay at your house for the weekend. Not now, since I'll be taking your Monopoly set back to my house after we finish the next game."

Sandra dealt bank money for the third game with a face like a storm, but her mother came and told them they must get into bed and put the light out, and she didn't take any notice of Sandra's howls and pleas for extra time. "We're going into town tomorrow," she said firmly. "So you both must get some sleep."

"We'll play that third game when we get back from town," said Sandra. "And I'll win it, and then you'll have to give me those playing cards. So I guess I just might be able to stand having you share my room for one night."

But Mary-Anna found that it was cozy to have someone else in the room at night, though she didn't tell Sandra that. She was scared of the dark as well as of horses, and at her own house her mother always let her leave the door open. Having someone actually sleeping in the same room was even better, even if that person was an enemy. She had to admit to herself that the enemy's solid shape under the blankets in the other bed was comforting, and so was the sound of her breathing.

4 Disaster at the Museum

"I have to do some shopping in town," Mrs. Sutton said in the morning. "But we'll have time to visit the museum, too. Sandra, you're not wearing that silly-looking jockey cap. Take it off right now."

As soon as she had heard that they were going to the museum where they could see Phar Lap, Sandra had put on her jockey cap. One of the main attractions at the museum was a model of a famous racehorse called Phar Lap. Sandra's jockey cap was an old plastic crash helmet covered with pictures of horses. It looked pretty weird, but Sandra liked people to think that she might own a horse. "Can I just carry it, then?" she asked.

"No, you can't," said Mrs. Sutton. "Mary-Anna looks nice and neat to go into town. Why don't you try to be as neat as Mary-Anna?"

In the train, Sandra didn't take the seat next to Mary-Anna. She sat opposite and scowled out the window. Mary-Anna did the same. Once, when Sandra's shoe accidentally brushed against hers, she jerked her foot back as though Sandra's shoe had the measles. "Really, you two are too much!" Mrs. Sutton said.

While Mrs. Sutton did her shopping, Mary-Anna and Sandra trailed behind looking at window displays privately and separately. Sandra didn't call Mary-Anna when she found a pet-store window, and Mary-Anna didn't show her a model alpine village she found in a travel-agency window. And when they got to the museum, they did the same.

"Why did we have to come in by this

door?" said Sandra. "I wanted to see Phar Lap first. He's the best thing in this museum. I wish they'd take him out of that glass display case and let kids sit on him."

"He's not real," said Mary-Anna. "It's just his skin filled with Play-Doh or Plasticine or something. And with glass eyes."

"So what?" demanded Sandra. "He's still the best thing in this museum. You don't want to see him because you're scared of horses. Even a plaster one with the skin sewn on and glass eyes, you're still scared of that. What a jerk!"

"Sandra, don't talk that way!" Mrs. Sutton scolded. "And I think you should let Mary-Anna choose what she wants to look at first. She's your guest."

"No, she isn't," muttered Sandra. "I never asked her to stay at our house."

To pay her back, Mary-Anna asked if they could go upstairs and look at the rock specimens, because she knew Sandra thought they were boring. She spent ages going from one rock cabinet to another, reading the information on every little card straight through. She worked her way slowly along one side. "Oh, goody," she said, glancing at Sandra. "There's a whole lot more over on that side. Hundreds of them."

"I don't want to look at any more old rock samples," said Sandra. "Can't I go downstairs and look at Phar Lap on my own?"

"No, you can't," said Mrs. Sutton. "You have to stay together where I can see you both. It's easy to get lost and separated in town. Wait till Mary-Anna finishes looking at her rocks."

Mary-Anna lingered, and even borrowed a pen and a piece of paper from Mrs. Sutton and wrote down things about opals. "There's a fossil collection over there we missed," she said.

"I want to see Phar Lap!" Sandra hollered, and several people turned and looked at her, shocked, while a guard near the door frowned at her for making a noise like that

in the museum. Mrs. Sutton was embarrassed to have a child who had to be frowned at by the museum guard, and she told Sandra indignantly to behave herself.

"You can just wait till Mary-Anna and I have a look at the engines," she said. "The idea, carrying on like that in a public place! Mary-Anna's being good and looking at everything properly. So why can't you do the same? Be a nice girl like Mary-Anna."

Sandra made private vomiting noises. Mary-Anna was looking at a model of a coal mine, and Sandra went around to the other side of the glass case and waited till Mary-Anna noticed her. Then she squashed her mouth into an oblong, slobbered against the glass, and pulled down her bottom eyelids and showed the red linings. A guard walking past said, "Hey, you! Don't touch the glass like that!" and Mrs. Sutton looked humiliated and yelled at Sandra again.

Mary-Anna was having a fantastic time seeing Sandra get into trouble.

"Now can we go see Phar Lap?" Sandra demanded sulkily.

"Could I please go to the bathroom first, Mrs. Sutton?" Mary-Anna asked. She really did want to, but Sandra glared at her fiercely, imagining that she was just thinking up ways to postpone Phar Lap.

"We might as well all go," said Mrs. Sutton.

"Not me," said Sandra. "I'm not coming. I'll go and look at Phar Lap and wait for you."

Mrs. Sutton's feet were hurting from walking from one display to another, and she said more snappily than she intended, "For heaven's sake, Sandra, didn't I tell you we all had to stay together? Am I talking ancient Egyptian or something? You're not to get out of my sight for one minute. My goodness, but you're a pain in the neck today! Why can't you behave as nicely as Mary-Anna? You're coming along to the bathroom whether you need to or not. And one more word out of you, and you won't be allowed to see Phar Lap at all!"

"It's not fair!" Sandra muttered. "I don't see why I have to be dragged along to the ladies' room just because Mary-Anna Clutterworth needs to go. She's the pain in the neck, not me."

"Sandra, what did I just tell you?" Mrs. Sutton said sharply.

"It's yucky enough having to sit next to her at school. I certainly don't want her and her stupid old dragon nightgown cluttering up my room over the weekend. I wish she'd gone to Sydney for her stupid old uncle's wedding. It's a wonder he found anyone to marry him, seeing he's related to Mary-Anna Clutterworth. Maybe that's why he didn't invite her, so he could keep her out of sight till the bride said yes."

"Right," said Mrs. Sutton. "No Phar Lap."

Sandra shut up, too late, and looked as though she might start to bawl. But instead she shot Mary-Anna a terrible, threatening,

I'll-get-even look. Mary-Anna felt uncomfortable and guilty. Sandra had twenty-three postcard pictures of Phar Lap stuck on her bedroom door and nine large ones on the wall above her bed. The museum sold them at the entrance desk, and every time a class from school went to the museum, Sandra gave them some of her pocket money to buy her more photos. She didn't mind that they were all the same. She was trying to get into the *Guinness Book of World Records,* as well as decorate all her walls and the ceiling and the floor, too, with pictures of Phar Lap.

Mary-Anna tugged at Mrs. Sutton's sleeve. "Please let Sandra have a look at Phar Lap on the way out," she whispered.

"That's very nice of you, Mary-Anna," Mrs. Sutton said. "But I warned and warned Sandra, and she has only herself to blame. I can't give in to her at the last minute. Come on, let's go and find somewhere to have lunch."

Sandra marched stonily past store windows

with a scrunched-up face, and every time Mrs. Sutton and Mary-Anna stopped to admire something, Sandra stared up at the sky.

It was difficult to find somewhere to eat because it was lunchtime for all the other shoppers, too, and all the cafés and take-out places were crowded. They walked along the main shopping streets and through a maze of arcades, and finally found a cafeteria down in the basement of one of them.

Mary-Anna offered to pay for her lunch, because her mother had given her some extra money for the weekend. But Mrs. Sutton said to keep it for spending money. "Buy Sandra a nice, new, smiling, pleasant face," she said. Sandra heard and scowled even more into her chocolate shake. When Mary-Anna sat down next to her, she slid her tray to the farthest edge of the table and moved herself along after it, so that a lot of her was hanging over into the aisle.

Mrs. Sutton had only a little plate of cottage cheese and lettuce and a cup of black coffee because she was on a diet. She ate her lunch very slowly so that her stomach would be tricked into believing that it had been fed an enormous, lengthy meal. She still hadn't finished when Mary-Anna's and Sandra's trays were a litter of empty paper plates and paper napkins and milk-shake straws.

"I need to go to the bathroom," Sandra said urgently.

"Well, you had the chance to go at the museum, so now you'll just have to wait. You can't go off by yourself."

"I'll go with her," Mary-Anna offered. "There's a ladies' room sign over by the door."

"I don't need *you* to come with me," Sandra said spitefully.

"And I don't want you traipsing off on your own," said Mrs. Sutton. "You can both go, and stay together, and don't talk to strangers. I'm going to have another cup of coffee."

The ladies' room sign pointed down a double flight of steps, then along a passage and up another staircase. Sandra ignored Mary-Anna and took a long time in the bathroom on purpose. She even brushed her hair, slowly and carefully, and she washed her hands and dried them under the hot-air blower several times. Mary-Anna washed her hands, too, because the blower felt interesting. If she were ever rich, she decided, she would have a hot-air blower, a human-body-sized one, installed in her bathroom right next to the shower.

"Hurry up," Sandra ordered bossily. "I'm not hanging around waiting for you, Miss Goody-goody."

They went out the door and down the first flight of steps, along a passage, and up some more steps. Then they opened a door that should have led them back into the cafeteria, but there was just another corridor. "We've gone the wrong way," Mary-Anna said.

"No we haven't, stupid. There's the cafeteria door." Sandra pushed open a swinging

51

door at the end of the passage, and Mary-Anna followed her through it. But it led into a busy arcade.

"I told you it was the wrong door," said Mary-Anna. "What happened is we must have gone around in a circle to the front of the cafeteria. That glass door over there has to be the front door."

They opened it, but the glass door led into another shopping mall.

"Maybe it's at the end of this row of stores," said Sandra, and they walked down the mall, which branched into several arcades, all going off in different directions like the arms of an octopus. And by the time they finished inspecting the third one, they were lost. They tried to go back to the starting point, but something seemed to have happened to the arrangement of doors, passages, stairs, and stores, and everything looked completely different. Mary-Anna and Sandra remembered that their mothers always said about a hundred times, every time they came into town, "If you get lost, just stand where you are and wait. Don't walk on and don't talk to strangers."

So they stood against the window of a fur store and waited for Mrs. Sutton to finish her coffee and come and find them.

5 All's Well That Ends Well

The fur-store window was a spooky thing to look at while they were waiting to be found. The furs hung on gold-painted plastic figures without heads, and inside the store it was hushed and dim and shadowy.

"Maybe those furs turned into animals again and ate up all the salesladies," Mary-Anna said nervously.

"The only fur coat that would be any good," said Sandra, "would be one made out of Phar Lap, if the museum would sell him. If I had Phar Lap for a fur coat, I'd wear him to the races. I think he'd like that. He wouldn't mind being a fur coat and going to the races again, because it must get boring inside that glass case."

They edged along to the next window, which had ballet shoes and tights and leotards. Sandra didn't like looking at leotards. "We have to wear them in exercise class," she said gloomily. "Mine's purple, and it makes me look like a big grape. And I can't do any of those exercises, anyhow. I can't even do things on the monkey bars at school."

"You should practice," said Mary-Anna. "Come one day and I'll show you. It's easy, if you practice." She was feeling kindly toward Sandra because they were both lost and worried together.

"Can you remember what that cafeteria was called?" asked Sandra. "We could ask someone the way there."

But Mary-Anna couldn't remember, and besides, for years they had been told so

many times not to talk to strangers that everyone passing seemed vaguely threatening, even babies in strollers.

"We can't just stand here all weekend," said Sandra. "I think we should walk around and look for that cafeteria some more."

They walked in and out of arcades, but not one of them had a cafeteria. Every time they saw a woman wearing a white jacket and a navy skirt, their spirits soared. But it always turned out to be someone else, and not Sandra's mother. Mary-Anna began to feel angry with everyone she saw dressed like that, as though they had all gotten up that morning and put on a white jacket and a skirt just like Mrs. Sutton's, and had gone to town on purpose just to confuse Sandra and her.

"Maybe your mom has gone back to the museum to look for us," she suggested. "She might think we went back there to look at Phar Lap."

"Who cares about Phar Lap?" Sandra said unhappily. She would never have said such a terrible, insulting thing about Phar Lap if she hadn't been lost and scared and miserable.

"Well, she might think that," Mary-Anna persisted.

"All right, then, we'll go back to the museum, but we'll have to ask someone the way."

They looked around for a policeman to ask, but the only one they could find was out in the middle of an intersection directing traffic, and he looked much too busy to disturb.

"Let's ask at that newsstand," Sandra said.

"He's a stranger," said Mary-Anna.

"But I don't think he'd kidnap us so close to the policeman."

The man at the newsstand showed them how to get to the museum, which wasn't very far away. Mrs. Sutton wasn't there looking for them, but they stood hopefully just inside the main door and watched for a white jacket and a navy skirt.

"While we're waiting for your mom to find us, you could have a really good look at Phar Lap," Mary-Anna said.

So they found their way to the section where he was, and Sandra inched around Phar Lap's case for several slow, worshiping, clockwise turns, and then five counterclockwise ones. "Oh," she said softly, "I just wish I'd been Phar Lap's jockey or even the person who sold him his oats. Or even the person who made the nails for his shoes."

Before they became lost, Mary-Anna might have remarked that clumsy people couldn't ever be jockeys, but she was beginning to feel quite differently toward Sandra now. It was as though she and Sandra were adrift together on a raft with sharks slicing the ocean around them. Mary-Anna realized suddenly that they had been drifting around the city for nearly two hours, and in that time they hadn't said one nasty thing to each other, which was remarkable.

And while Sandra was still at the glass

case, dreamy with admiration, Mary-Anna slipped away and went to the desk and bought a photo of Phar Lap. She put it in her bag without Sandra noticing.

There were plenty of other mothers coming in and out of the museum, but Sandra's didn't come. "I guess we'll just have to find our own way home on the train," Sandra said. "We'd better do that and wait at my house in case Mom calls. We'll have to use your weekend money. Do you know the way to the station?"

Mary-Anna thought hard. "When we came this morning, we walked in a straight line, and I think the station was at the end of the straight line, only on the other side of the street. But it's so big I don't think we could go past it by accident."

The straight line was a much longer one than they remembered.

"I never had to buy a train ticket on my own before," Sandra said when they finally got there. "I don't know what to ask for."

"We're half-fare," said Mary-Anna. "And Mom always buys something called 'off peak,' so we'd better ask for that." Sandra was glad that she had Mary-Anna along, because the man behind the ticket counter wasn't very pleasant or friendly. He looked like a large, angry animal with a headache, in a cage.

"Two half-fares off peak where?" he growled. "Hurry up. I haven't got all day."

"To Glendale," Mary-Anna said quickly, put the money on the counter, and picked up the tickets. She started to walk away, and the man called impatiently, "Wait for the change, can't you, kid!"

"He's got nerve to talk to us like that," Mary-Anna said indignantly. "We're customers of the railroad. He should be more polite."

"Customers of the railroad" sounded very grand. Actually, she had often thought that it must feel important to pass through a turnstile without your mother or another adult,

but now that she was having the chance it just felt scary. Usually you just followed your mother, and she always knew exactly which ramp to go down. Following Sandra wasn't nearly as easy. For a start, she was just as lost as Mary-Anna and apparently just as confused by all the signs above the ramps.

People jostled them with elbows and shopping bags. And in one terrible moment, Sandra was snatched away out of sight by the stream of people. Mary-Anna was so tired she could hardly bear it, and losing Sandra was unbelievable. She stepped out of the tidal wave and found a safe bay of newspaper stands. She struggled not to cry, but her chin was starting to wobble. Everything was horrible; no Mrs. Sutton, and no Sandra, and two tickets in her hand, and no idea of which ramp to go down.

And suddenly there was Sandra, and she looked as dependable and friendly as a little tugboat. "Mary-Anna, don't look like that," she said. "Come on, I know which way to go. I found the right sign."

Mary-Anna whisked away her tears, and when they were walking down the ramp she reached over and took Sandra's hand and started to swing their two arms, the way kids who were friends did on Mr. Morley's nature-study walks.

There was a train to Glendale just about to leave, and when it had traveled through several stations with familiar-sounding names, Mary-Anna felt very much better. She took out the photograph of Phar Lap and gave it to Sandra. "It's for you," she said. "I don't collect horse pictures. I'm scared of horses. Did that horse really chase some kid and stomp on her foot and refuse to get off?"

Sandra told her she'd only made that up. "That old horse never chases anyone. You don't have to be scared of him. I go in there lots of times and feed him apples."

She thought it was odd that Mary-Anna

could do so many risky, clever things on the jungle gym, and still be scared of a quiet old horse. And Mary-Anna was thinking that it was funny that Sandra should be scared of climbing up the bars when she wasn't the least bit afraid of getting close to a horse.

It wasn't a long walk from the Glendale station to Sandra's house, but it felt neverending to feet that had been lost and walking all over the city. Sandra got the spare key to the front door. It was hidden in a very good place, taped underneath the bowl of the birdbath in the middle of the lawn.

The telephone was ringing and ringing as they walked in, and there was a very worried Mrs. Sutton on the other end. She'd been looking for the girls for hours and had been walking all over town just as much as they had, only in different places at different times. Otherwise, they would have found each other. She said she had been back to the museum again, and the man at the desk had remembered Mary-Anna buying the picture of Phar Lap. "So I thought, if you managed to find the museum again, you might have found your way back to the station as well."

"We were okay because Sandra knew which platform," Mary-Anna said. Mrs. Sutton wanted to speak to her on the phone, too, just to make sure she was safe. She half thought that Sandra might have arranged to lose Mary-Anna in the city permanently.

"And we were okay because Mary-Anna knew which tickets to ask for," Sandra said, taking the phone back. "We'll get dinner ready if you want to stay in town and finish your shopping."

Mary-Anna felt a warm glow when she said that, because usually she and Sandra were never a "we." It seemed much more sensible to be "we" when their mothers were like that, too, and went to tennis and yoga and the night shift at the hospital together.

So Mary-Anna set the table while Sandra made a fruit salad for dinner. She made an

unusual one, adding crumbled-up gingersnaps to the fruit, as well as sprinkles and apricot jam and some cream cheese left over in the refrigerator. And after that was done, they had time to finish the third Monopoly game.

They still squabbled when they played, and Sandra said, "Right. I'm going to get you, Mary-Anna Clutterworth!" when Mary-Anna won. But she didn't sound as fierce as usual! She gave Mary-Anna's wooden puzzle back. "You may as well keep it," she said. "It's too easy for me."

Mary-Anna could have claimed the Monopoly set, but she decided to leave it at Sandra's place. They both thought it would be silly carrying it back and forth from one house to the other, when they would be playing Monopoly every day after school at Sandra's house, anyway.